Now You Can Lay Me Down to Sleep

If I Shall Die before I Wake!

CHERITA FORD

Copyright © 2021 Cherita Ford
All rights reserved
First Edition

PAGE PUBLISHING, INC.
Conneaut Lake, PA

First originally published by Page Publishing 2021

ISBN 978-1-64544-150-2 (pbk)
ISBN 978-1-64544-149-6 (digital)

Printed in the United States of America

Chapter 1

Now Lay Me Down to Sleep

Late 1800s…

It's the late 1800s, and the winds are strong and fierce as the older boys gather up all the family's farm animals to place them inside the family's barn in small town Woodstock, New York. Barely able to see within the darkness, the boys twelve, fifteen, and sixteen years old are working hard to gather up the family animals as they all scatter from fear of the stronger than normal winds in their small town. Charlie, the youngest of the four boys, stand in the doorway of his small old house watching his older brothers as they're running all around, trying to catch the animals. Turning quickly, Charlie is startled and turns his head toward a gentle tap on his right shoulder. He realizes it's his mother. He looks up at her. His mother may have had four kids, but with her four-foot-eleven height and 110 pounds frame, you could never guess it. In fact, a lot of the towns woman dislikes her because of it.

"Charlie honey, it's time for you to wash up and then say your prayers before bed," says his mother in a very soft-spoken tone of voice. Looking up at his thin-framed mother in her beautiful blue eyes, smiling, then turning around, he immediately runs and follows her orders.

After Charlie puts on his folded red pajamas that his mother has placed on the foot of his neatly made bed, he then slowly bends down gets to his knees, puts his tiny hands together at the foot of his bed. Charlie shuts his eyes tightly as possible like he has always done in the past when saying his prayers before bed.

"Now I lay me down to sleep. I pray the Lord my soul to keep. If I shall die before I wake, I pray the Lord my soul to take," Charlie says.

Before he opens his eyes, he feels a bitter cold breeze all over his itty-bitty body. As the tiny bumps on his arms rise, he starts to feel each of the hairs on his arms gently lifts with the unusual still cold breeze while it sweeps across each hair at a leisurely pace. Suddenly his little body jerks with one solid quick shock, and then abruptly his brown eyes open wide, turning his sclera, pupil, and iris ink-black. Charlie is slow to get up off his knees and onto his feet. After standing up, he immediately lies on top of his perfectly made bed, keeping his eyes open and never getting underneath his sheets. He's listening as his three older brothers and parents are finally settling down for the night.

With the house now silent, Charlie gently gets out of his bed and calmly walks step by step into his family's barn, grabs his family's ax, and slowly he grips the heavy ax tightly in his tiny right hand. His body feels like it has been sitting in a giant bucket of ice cubes in the middle of one of Alaska's ice-cold blizzard. Step by step, Charlie gradually moves closer toward his house. He stares at the tiny barn-shaped figure as he approaches it within the darkness inch by inch. The atmosphere outside makes the surroundings seems to be darker than usual. Charlie counts the steps one at a time, "One…two… three…four." As he marches step by step…Charlie's tone of voice becomes more sinister with every step leading up to his front door. Suddenly he stops counting once he reaches the eighth unstable wooden step that leads to the old slab of wood that is placed on top of a mound of rocks and dirt. As his left foot hits the top of his home-made porch first, he never loses his balance; that is not the norm for young Charlie because of the unstableness in the way the large thick slab of wood has started to curve just a little bit due to the weather. Charlie never blinks. He's gripping the ax in his tiny hand tighter and tighter. Slowly he reaches his left arm out, turns the doorknob until the door finally opens to enter into his house.

Once inside, he heads straight toward his parents' room first. Standing over his parents, gawking at them for a few seconds, he watches at his mother as she lies peacefully cuddled in his father's arms. His eyes shifts satanically. Then without warning, Charlie lifts the heavy ax above his head; the heavy ax is as light as a feather to him. After a burst of energy, he suddenly feels his parents warm blood all over his small body as it scatters everywhere. The ax chops off his dad's head, and his mom is sliced in half from the shoulders up. Just like that, not a sound, Charlie then turns, walks out his parents' room at a steady, creepy, slow-moving pace, never blinking, he appears in his two older brothers' room, standing in between their bed that is directly across from one another.

"Charlie, what are you doing?" asks his oldest brother, turning and waking up to see Charlie is bloody and holding the ax over him. Swiftly Charlie swings his ax at high speed, chopping him up into chunks. Then quickly he slaughters his other two brothers, leaving his whole family dead in their tiny house. Done, he walks back out the house, drops his bloody ax, then slowly and calmly walks into the woods till a short time later.

"His mother was a bloody whore who had a house filled with the little ankle bitters, I tell you," says Mrs. Smith. Looking down at Charlie with his brown, medium-length bedhead hair and his brown eyes that have now turned completely black. Mrs. Smith can't help but notice his frail pale skin.

Charlie's eyes are glued on her medium-build body frame and her all-white dress and boots; he observes how her hair is black and neatly swept back like his mother wore hers. The little boy bows his head so that they can't see his dirty eight-year-old bloodless face.

"Well, do you think he may have that green fever?" asks Mrs. Moore as she stares down at Charlie with his legs still tucked underneath him.

"Bloody no, he ain't got no greensickness that's for sure. If he had anemia, his iron would be low, and he would be cold out here in the darkness," response Mrs. Smith.

"Maybe he may have that Black Death plague then," Mrs. Moore suggests.

"Maybe," Mrs. Smith replies, frowning down at Charlie.

"Whose boy is this?" asks Mrs. Moore.

"The Minks. That family killed by an ax murderer about a week ago. This is the child that was said to be missing everyone is on the hunt for," explains Mrs. Smith.

"Oh yes, I can remember now," says Mrs. Moore.

Charlie keeps his head down and his knees firmly tucked underneath him.

"What's your name... Is it Charlie?" asks Mrs. Moore, holding back her blond straight hair with her right hand to keep it from falling within her face as she bends to get a closer look at Charlie as she bends to get down close to him. She bends enough without getting to her knees.

Charlie never says a word, nor does he look back up at the two women. Gazing down at the ground, Charlie thinks it's best to just let the two ladies talk to one another.

"Are you at sea on thinking, you little bugger?" asks Mrs. Smith as she lifts her feet up off the ground and kicks him hard with her black, shiny boots.

"Yes, his name is Charlie. I remember him now. He was the youngest of the Minks boys. Didn't you hate his mother?" asks Mrs. Moore as she raises back up straight, still looking down in Charlie's direction.

Mrs. Smith looks at Mrs. Moore with a bug-eyed, dark look, then they both look back down at Charlie.

"Well, if you are to be around here at the orphanage, you will have to bone up like everyone else around here," she says.

NOW YOU CAN LAY ME DOWN TO SLEEP

"That's right. No child lives here without putting in hard work," Mrs. Moore agrees. She reaches her hand out, tapping Charlie on the top of the head. Looking up at her, he sees she waves her hand in a get-up-come-with-me motion.

Charlie slowly gets up off the ground with his red pajamas covered in blood and begins to follow walking, still not saying a word, walking up the long stairs and into the hospital-looking institution.

"Here's the bathroom, and here's some washcloths plus your clothes for the night," says Mrs. Smith as she shoves the items into Charlie's chest and arms.

After washing up and putting on the clean rags, the boy slowly walks out the bathroom.

"Charlie," Mrs. Smith says, still standing in the hall with her arms folded, waiting on him to be done.

Looking at Mrs. Smith with a blank stare, Charlie slowly walks toward her.

"You will sleep in here, Charlie, with the other boys," she says then opens the door to a room filled with two rows of beds along each the walls and boys down on their knees as if they were waiting to be told they could talk or move. Charlie looks as each boy has their hands together waiting to pray.

"Okay, your bed is the third one on the left," says Mrs. Smith, pointing at the empty bed neatly made with white sheets and one single pillow on it. Charlie looks at each boy as he walks to his assigned bed and gets to his knees and puts his hands together.

"Okay, boys, you can begin now," says Mrs. Smith.

"Now lay me down to sleep. I pray the Lord my soul to keep. If should die before I wake, I pray the Lord my soul to take," Mrs. Smith and all the boys except Charlie recite at the same time, and then they climb into their beds.

"Charlie, come here now. Why come you didn't recite your bedtime prayer?" she asks furiously.

Charlie doesn't say a word as he walks up to Mrs. Smith. She snatches him by his shirt collar and pulls him out of the room. "I see. I need to teach you a lesson already," she says, as she closes the door, shoving him to the ground as hard as she could. She then walks over

7

to her hall closet, grabbing her wooden stick, walking back toward Charlie. She raises her arm and hand as far back as she can, swinging and hitting Charlie as many times as she can in a few minutes. Charlie withstands as many hits as she puts out before he stands to his feet, grabbing her stick, snatching and breaking it into two pieces. Charlie then grins and takes the stick stabs her in the back, and she falls to the ground screaming and yelling in agony pain. Then he picks up a very tiny piece of the stick he has broken and shoves it into her forehead, killing her with her eyes and mouth still wide open. Quickly, Charlie places his hand on her dead body, taking her soul as blood pours out from her forehead and courses from her back. Charlie violently kills each and everyone in the orphanage that night, and the next morning, he jumps onto the orphanage train that is transporting thirty children and three adults. Charlie looked around the train as he takes a seat as fast as his little feet and legs carry him. Then he feels the train start to take off. A lot of the children gives Charlie the evil eye because of the blood splatter stains on his clothes. Keeping his head down, Charlie tries to hope that the movement of the train will take the unwanted focus of him. The kids for the most part swiftly shift the attention on the men outside working on the railroad, and the train takes off.

"Why do you have blood on your unmentionables?" says a voice coming from the little, round sweet face, a big brown-eyed, straight- and blond-haired little girl seated next to Charlie. Charlie doesn't speak or blink even. He keeps his head down and has a bleak look on his face, hoping she'd simply shut up.

"My name is Martha. Guess how old I am. I'm eight," she quickly tells Charlie, looking at him and then smiling.

Charlie stays mute. He never even blinks. As the train continues to move at its regular speed, Charlie's body moves a little from side to side, both his arms stay down to his side as hands are spread across the seat. Martha can't take her eyes off of Charlie. She watches as one of the female adults that are helping watch over the children above the train comes walking over to Charlie. The lady bends downward just enough to talk to Charlie and not have to yell over the sound of the train and the other children above the train.

NOW YOU CAN LAY ME DOWN TO SLEEP

"Hello, little one, what's your name?" the female adult asks Charlie, placing her left hand gently on Charlie's right shoulder.

Charlie never looks up at her once.

"Are you okay? You feel cold?" she asks as she looks down at Charlie's blood-splattered clothes.

"I'm fine," Charlie response in very low sotto voice.

"He's fine. He's my brother. He's just a little poked up right now," Martha quickly response as she's leaning and looking over past Charlie so that she and the lady are staring eye to eye. The lady gives Martha a look of doubt as she raises up and then takes her hand off of Charlie's shoulder.

"Have you both been arranged to go out west to the same farm family?" asks the lady.

"Yes," says Martha. She then hugs Charlie for a few seconds with her right arm and afterward quickly and gently fixes his windswept hair with her right hand. Martha looks up and cracks a half smile at the lady worker. As the lady smiles back, she turns and walks away. She never notices that Charlie is the boy who is said to have done a massacre on his whole family, and the story is all over the New York paper. Once in Indiana, Martha and Charlie are placed at a farm to do work like a lot of the homeless and neglected children on the New York streets. As night falls, the farm family that takes Charlie and Martha in say their prayers before bed. Martha refuses to do so because she is never taught to say a bedtime prayer, but she does get down on her knees and folds her hands together like everyone else, even Charlie. Martha just listens as the other recite the words to the prayer.

"Now lay me down to sleep. I pray the Lord my soul to keep. If I shall die before I wake, I pray the Lord my soul to take," the farm family all say before bed.

Charlie goes into the owners of the house bedroom, grabs a rifle that is leaned up against the wall, and then grabs bullets from the wooden box placed on the floor. With the gun in his hands, he walks calmly into each room, shooting and killing. He slowly walks through the house and stands at each one of seven out of eight people that consist of the two adults and their five orphanage children, killing them all with an 1861 Bridesburg rifle musket. Police find and kill Charlie in the woods that night by burning him alive, and his funeral is short and brief. Everyone is glad the sinful corrupted soul of Charlie Minks is finally dead. Everyone but Martha, he has left her alive, and she grieves his death until she dies thirty years later in her Missouri home from silage that would form a gas that would suck the oxygen out of her lungs, and she suffocates.

I pray the Lord my soul to keep!

125 years later...

Hundred years later, in a small town called St. Charles in the state of Missouri, Skyler stares at her many beautiful dollhouses. Each one is different with little dolls that fit so perfectly inside their designated spots, and all twenty-two of her rare dollhouses make up a unique village. For as long as she can remember, her grandparents have bought her a beautiful dollhouse as a gift for each birthday and Christmas of her life, and in a few days, it will be June 18. Skyler is turning a teenager.

"Your dollhouses are so awesome, Skyler. I wish my grandparents would have filled me a room with such lovely dollhouses that are replicates of a real-life village," says Cora, Skyler's friend.

"Yeah, well, I am turning thirteen this year. I don't think I want another dollhouse that I'm not going to play with," says Skyler. As she gazes around her playroom that sits across from her small bedroom, she thinks to herself how she wishes her parents would get rid of her many dollhouses and change the playroom into her bedroom because it's much bigger than the room she sleeps in.

"Well, I've seen a very beautiful dollhouse at the antique store around the corner by my house that I would love for my parents to buy me," says Cora. She then cracks a smile and walks over to the large green-and-yellow dollhouse flopping down directly in front of it crossing her legs. With her big, blue eyes open wide, she reaches into the three-story four-room dollhouse and picks up the little girl doll, then picking up the tiny brush off the dresser and began gently brushing the dolls long blond hair.

"That's my favorite dollhouse. Everything in it reminds me of my house. That doll you're holding reminds me of me to-a-tee. Look at her long blond hair and her huge blue eyes," says Skyler, smiling, looking over and down at Cora.

"Skyler, last I checked your eyes are brown, and your hair is long and black," says Cora as she looks up and over at Skyler, then they both bust out and giggle loudly.

"Well, I'm sure my grandparents had me in mind when they purchased it," responds Skyler.

"That dollhouse at the antique mall is so perfect. It's packed with old-looking furniture, but there aren't any dolls in it," says Cora.

"Mmmm, that's strange. There were no dolls as part of the accessories in dollhouse?" question Skyler.

"But it is the most beautiful dollhouse I have ever laid eyes on," says Cora as she places the little doll and his brush neatly back into its place in the dollhouse.

"I just hope my grandparents don't decide that another freakin' dollhouse will be a good idea for my birthday present this year," says Skyler, walking up to her store dollhouse. She bends down and grabs the old-man doll from behind the counter, pulling him out the store. Then she places him into the little, blue toy car that sits on the floor in front of the dollhouse.

"You know, Skyler, I think this is wonderful what your grandparents have done. Don't be so selfish thinking about what you want. It's the thought that counts, and it's as if you have your own village right here in one room," says Cora, getting up off the floor and brushing her pants off with her hands before walking back over near Skyler, who is now standing in the middle of the huge room by her store dollhouse.

"Yep, one that I have outgrown, and I'm sick of," says Skyler as she bends down to place her old man doll in his toy car and then standing straight up stepping over him almost crushing him with the heel of her left red-and-white tennis shoe.

"But look at this place, you have a dollhouse collection that a little girl could only dream of as a kid, for example, a gas station dollhouse, the big red barn with all the animals and hay. You also have a mall dollhouse with all the workers plus merchandise. How many girls have a mall dollhouse with all the accessories to it?" explains Cora.

"Skyler!" Skyler's mother, Amber, yells as she walks up the steps headed their way.

"Yes, Mom, we're in here," response Skyler.

"Skyler honey, it's time to go to the dinner party that your aunt and uncle are throwing for your cousin Beach," Skyler's mother reminds her, walking into the playroom and stopping right at the entrance. She never comes all the way into the dollhouse room because of her fear of dolls being possessed. Her mother watches an old show called *Tales of the Crypt*, and the dolls from an old dollhouse come alive and start killing everyone. Skyler's mother then walks over and surprisingly picks the old man doll up out his car straightening his white apron before she places him back into his spot behind the store counter.

Skyler, smiling big, bucks her eyes and raises her eyebrow at her mother.

"Mom, you never come in here. What's gotten into you?" she asks.

"Well, normally I wouldn't come in here, but you girls are in here. It's daylight," says Skyler's mom as she marches back toward the door of the room, turns in the direction to face both girls.

Skyler is smiling ear to ear because she loves going to her uncle and aunt's house to see their fourteen-year-old daughter, Beach. Beach is her first cousin and best friend in the whole world other than Cora. Everyone that knows Beach and Skyler all says the two looks just alike. Skyler thinks she's more of a mini me of her mother, and Beach is her aunt Erma's twin. It's so hard for Skyler to see that she and her cousin have the look-alike factor. Although Skyler's mother and her aunt Erma are identical twins, but Skyler has long black shiny hair brown eyes and a slim-framed body while her cousin Beach weighs a little more and has blonde wavy hair and glasses.

"Mom, can Cora come to Beach's house with us? Please, please," begs Skyler.

"She has to call her mother first, Skyler, and ask permission, and I need to ask your aunt Erma if it's okay to bring someone extra along," explains her mother.

"Okay, call your mom, Cora, and ask can you come," says Skyler.

Cora immediately takes her cell phone out her pocket and calls her mother.

"She gave me the green light to go and have fun, guys," says Cora then smiling big.

After Skyler's mother confirmed that her aunt Erma said sure it's okay for Cora to come along, Skyler, her parents, and Cora head to her aunt Erma and uncle Larry's house for the dinner party.

"Hey, kiddoes," says Aunt Erma as she stands at the front door to greet their arrival, smiling big at Skyler and Cora as she steps aside to let everyone enter. Then she hugs everyone right before Uncle Larry walks up. He gives Skyler's dad, Randy, a big handshake and briefly hugs her mother Amber then bends to kiss Skyler on the forehead.

"Hey, princess, how are you?" he asks then he raises up and draws his attention toward Cora.

"I'm good, Uncle Larry," says Skyler smiling.

"Who's your friend?" asks her uncle Larry while the four adults stand and stare over and down at Cora. Skyler is thinking how odd Cora must be feeling right now with all these old folks gawking at her like she's about to recite "Windy Night," by Robert Louis Stevenson.

"My name is Cora. I live around the corner from Skyler, and we go to school together," says Cora then turning and looking at Skyler right before the both of them began leaning on one another snickering.

"Well, it's a pleasure to meet you, young lady," says Uncle Larry then he holds his hand out for a handshake.

"Oh," says Cora, and she holds her hand out grabbing his hand firmly, giving him a big up and down shake for a few seconds.

"Where is Beach?" asks Skyler.

"She is in the kitchen. Speaking of, let's go into the kitchen and all have a seat. Dinner is ready," says Aunt Erma then leading the group into the kitchen.

"Surprise!" a loud shout comes from a group of people. Skyler and Cora scream and jump after they enter the kitchen area.

"Oh my god, you guys scared the heck out of us," says Skyler, still holding her chest.

"Oh, sorry, dear, we apologize," says Skyler's grandmother.

"Wooh," says Skyler as she sees her whole family from her host of cousins to her grandparents on both side. She glances at all the purple and blue decorations hanging perfectly everywhere. Purple is her favorite color. She tries to by purple everything when she goes shopping.

"We've decided to surprise you and have your birthday dinner here early, sweetheart," says Skyler's dad.

"Hey, Skyler, happy birthday," says Beach, running up to Skyler then giving her a big, tight hug.

Skyler's whole family tells her happy birthday one at a time before they all sit down and eat to celebrate her birthday. After cake and ice cream, they all bring out their gifts they have brought. Cora calls her mom to rush her over a gift for Skyler. It was a beautiful friendship bracelet. Skyler receives such wonderful presents. Her aunt and uncle get her a designer purse, and her parents get her a credit card to her favorite store with a limit of five hundred dollars. She knows her dad's parents would get her a new nightgown and bed set and some house shoes to match. They always have since she has been big enough to remember.

"Dear, where is our gift?" asks her grandmother Ethal, her mom's mother, to her mom's father, Sie.

"It's in the car. Let me run and grab it," he says, moving as fast as he can before her dad jumps up quickly.

"I will go to get it, Sie," he says.

"Oh, okay, here's the keys. It's in the back seat wrapped very nicely," says her grandpa.

Holding his hand out, her dad grabs the keys and run out to get the gift. Skyler sits patiently, hoping it's not another dollhouse.

She is thinking to herself how she is going to lose her mind if she has to just stare at another huge dollhouse. Her dad reenters the house with a big, giant, long box. Skyler's stomach drops. Her dad places this humongous perfectly purple wrapped gift on the floor right in front of her whole family and Cora. They all watch as Skyler slowly unwraps the gorgeous paper that neatly covered it from one corner to the next. Once she pulls that one long piece that revealed what it is, she wants to scream. She sits with her mouth open for a few seconds.

"Thanks, Grandma and Grandpa," she says and then cracked a crooked grin.

"We hope you like it. We've seen it at the antique shop around the corner from your house. It was so beautiful we couldn't resist," says her grandmother Ethal.

Skyler gets up and gives each one of them a big hug.

"Wow, that's the dollhouse I was referring to," says Cora in an excited tone.

But all Skyler is thinking about is how she wasn't going to open it at all once she gets it home, or maybe she can push it out the car door while riding on the highway on the way home, and she then won't have to take it home at all.

"Skyler, would you like to have a sleepover tonight you, Cora, and Beach," says her mother, breaking the ice. She can tell that Skyler wasn't too excited to fill her hangout room with yet another dollhouse.

Once home, Skyler's dad takes the dollhouse into her playroom. He takes it out of the box then places it on the floor in the last empty spot left in the huge room. He can't help but think how different and impressive the new barn-house dollhouse looks compared to all the others. That night, Skyler, Cora, and Beach all have a blast. They bake cookies from scratch and do one another's hair and makeup. Then they watch a movie, eat popcorn and candy and drank soda till they have caffeine high. Beach gets up off the sofa and goes upstairs while Cora and Skyler are busy laughing at the movie. She hasn't been in Skyler's dollhouse room in a few weeks; she normally goes in there with Skyler, and she takes pictures to put on Instagram and Facebook so all her friends can see and give her lots of likes. Walking in the room, she turns on the light, and in amazement, the new dollhouse is stunning. It is old but very real-looking. Beach has never seen a dollhouse with such realistic features. Amazed, she begins flicking pictures of it to put online.

"What are you doing, Beach, trying to bail out on us?" says Skyler as she and Cora rush into the playroom giggling and shoving one other back and forth.

"Are you kidding me? I would pick this room rather than hang with you guys any day," Beach says jokingly as she straightens her glasses on her face.

"Let's go back downstairs," says Skyler.

And the three run down the steps as fast as they can before Skyler's mother, Amber, scolds them on running while on the stairs.

"Have you guys heard of the tale of the bedtime soul killer?" asks Skyler, looking at Beach and Cora smiling as the three sit on the couch to watch a movie.

"No," they both reply at the same time.

"Well, it is a story of a little boy possessed by an evil spirit, and he would come to kill and snatch souls from people that would say their prayers at night, but the spirit had to find a host to possess first, and it found a little boy named Charlie who became so evil he kills anyone that said the prayer, including his whole entire family," says Skyler.

"What would the prayer be, Skyler?" asks Beach.

"Well, I heard they would say, 'Now lay me down to sleep. I pray the Lord my soul to keep. If I should die before I wake, I pray the Lord my soul to take," says Skyler, and then she giggled.

Late before bed, Cora thought it would be funny to get down on her knees, close her eyes, and say the prayer. "Now lay me down to sleep. I pray the Lord my soul to keep. If I shall die before I wait, I pray the Lord my soul to take," says Cora then she opens her eyes.

"Oh my god, Cora, you said the prayer," says Beach, then looks over at Skyler, then bursts out laughing.

"Cora, now you're going to become possessed or something," says Skyler.

"I know. Now let's get some sleep," says Cora in a playful satanic tone of voice. Then the girls all giggle and settle down for the night.

"Good night, guys," says Skyler.

"Good night."

That night Skyler lies in her bed and thinks that she has shut the light off in her dollhouse room, but she can see that the light is on and shining right under the door of her room. Getting up out of bed, trying not to step on Cora or Beach as she tiptoes over each of them, Skyler walks quickly into the dollhouse room and flicks the light off, and for the first time, she sees and pays attention to her new dollhouse; her mouth drops. It's antique-looking but lights up on its own as if it has a sensor on it. It is beautiful, more so than all the other dollhouses in the room. Turning the light off, Skyler stands, staring at her new big barn-house dollhouse. All the windows in the house are as real-looking as the dollhouse itself. The tiny flowers that sit in front of the old steps that lead to the porch of the dollhouse also look real. Turning and walking out while flicking the lights on and off once more, Skyler walks off and stops instantly; her heart rate began to race rapidly and steady. She thinks she hears a faint giggle sound coming from within one of the dollhouses at that second. Skyler's heart is beating so loud she can hear it. Slowly turning back around, looking into the darkroom, she sees the lights on. The new dollhouse blinks a few seconds like a strobe light. Suddenly it stops and stays on. Skyler is standing, staring at the dollhouse, and sees nor hears nothing else strange coming from the room, and then she turns the light on and off once more and walks back into her room. She tiptoes back over the girls and quietly climbs back into her bed; then she closes her eyes and then falls fast asleep.

She hear a female's laughter.

Cora spontaneously opens her eyes. She lies on the floor in the darkness, staring at the blank wall straight across from her. Reaching over, she grabs her cell phone that's next to her pillow. She sees nothing but a small glare from the moonlight that's shining through the window of the bedroom.

She hear a female chuckle.

NOW YOU CAN LAY ME DOWN TO SLEEP

Cora instantly raises up and looks in the direction of the bedroom door. She slowly gets up from her bright-pink sleeping bag with her phone in her right hand.

Then the female chuckles once again.

Step by step, Cora begins to creep toward the direction of the sound. The room is silent and pitch-black as Cora lightly steps over Beach as she moves closer to the bedroom door. Putting her right hand on the doorknob slowly, she begins turning it until she can pull the door open. Across the hall, she can see the glow from the new dollhouse from her distance. Suddenly there's a tiny shadow that runs swiftly across the living room window of the dollhouse. Instantly, Cora's heart begins to pound so loud that she can hear it. As she eases closer toward the dollhouse room, she can feel her body getting hotter and hotter.

"Cora," whispers a soft-spoken female's voice from the dollhouse living room. Then the new dollhouse immediately lights up, blinking like a strobe light.

Cora walks at a slow-moving pace inch by inch until she is standing directly in between the doorway of Skyler's playroom. She's as stiff as a broad, staring at the new dollhouse without a blink. Her right hand shakes as her phone commences to vibrate. She holds her cell phone with a tight grip. Suddenly, out of nowhere, a wrinkled, white female's hand with sharp black nails comes from within the tiny living room window of the dollhouse. Cora's bright-green eyes are wide. She breathes heavily then inhales, and without warning, a magnetic field from the ghostly hand quickly sucks Cora into the dollhouse. Her phone hits the floor at the speed of lightning. The spot Cora once stood is empty, and not a sound can be heard within the darkness that lies inside the family's home. Then the lights in the new dollhouse all turn off at once.

The next morning, Beach is the first to be awakened with the good smell of bacon, eggs, french toast, and coffee. Getting up off the floor, she sees Cora's pink sleeping bag and that the bedroom door is open, but Skyler is still sleeping in her bed. Walking out of the bedroom, getting ready to go toward the bathroom down the hall, she stops, looks down, and in front of the doorway of the playroom, she sees Cora's cell phone. Beach bends down to pick it up and walks into the dollhouse room. All she sees is Skyler's dollhouse village; nothing seems out of place.

"Cora!" says Beach, looking around the room.

Beach then turns and quickly walks out and go to the bathroom to wash up for breakfast. Once downstairs, she goes past Skyler's dad, whose attention is locked into a laptop that sits on his lap as he relaxes in his favorite chair.

"Good morning, Uncle Randy," says Beach as her leg brushes up against his house shoes that are snugged on his feet dangling off the recliner.

Glancing up for just a few seconds, "Oh, good morning, my favorite niece," he says.

"Hey, Aunt Amber," Beach replies.

"Beach," says Skyler's mom, Amber.

"Did Cora leave to go home? Because I picked her cell phone up off the floor in the upstairs hallway by the playroom," says Beach. As she softly tosses the cell phone onto the table, it vibrates, and the name "My Beautiful Mom" pops up on the screen.

"Hello," answers Beach.

"Hey, let me speak with Cora. Who is this? Skyler?" asks Cora's mother.

"Oh, hey, Mrs. Church. No, it's Beach. I'm Skyler's cousin, and we were just looking for Cora. We thought maybe she went home," explains Beach.

Cora's mother quickly hangs up the cell phone.

"That was her mother, and she's on her way over. I think because Cora is not with her either," Beach says in a worried tone, looking over at her Aunt Amber.

"I have a horrible feeling about this," says Amber, running into the living room with her husband.

"What's wrong, honey? You look troubled," he tells her. Putting his paper down, he gets up and grabs her arms gently.

"It's Cora. She's not in the house, I don't think, or with her parents," says Amber frantically.

"What, wait, wait, let's not jump to conclusions. Let's first recheck the whole house before we come to that assumption," says Randy.

Beach runs upstairs as fast as possible to awake Skyler, and after telling her about Cora's disappearance, by the time the four of them have finished, her mother and father have arrived.

"Oh my god, I am so worried," says Cora's mom, Kat.

"I am so sorry, this is such a nightmare," says Amber.

"I'll call the police," says Randy.

After the police arrive, the house becomes chaotic, and things don't get halfway settled down till the police and Cora's and Beach's parents left. And now the police is finally done with their extensive search and plenty of questions that they have for everyone that is in the house that day, but now things seem to be more of a mystery to Cora's whereabouts than before.

If I shall die…

Chapter 3

It's late, Skyler and her parents decide to grab a bite to eat before coming back home to rest for the night. Things get bizarre. Louri, Randy's twenty-one-year-old daughter from a previous marriage, arrives from college unannounced.

"Mom, Dad, it's me Louri," she yells, walking throughout the house. After seeing there's no one home, she grabs her cellular out her purse and then texts her dad.

>
> LOURI. Dad it's me Louri… where are you guys?
> LOURI'S DAD. We are out to eat alot went on last-night and today huney
> LOURI. Well I'm in town for Beach's thirteenth birthday I thought it would be a great surprise to touch down in St. Charles from Michigan today
> LOURI'S DAD. We are on our way home now honey
> LOURI. Okay I love you guys
> LOURIE'S DAD. Love you too
> LOURI. ttyl dad

Exhausted, Louri decides to take a shower while the family is out to eat. After showering, she looks at her cellular phone and sees it's getting late. As she's walking past the room filled with dollhouses,

NOW YOU CAN LAY ME DOWN TO SLEEP

the blinking of the new barn-house dollhouse catches her attention. Stopping, she squinches her eyes. Gazing into the room and with vigilance, without hurrying, with one foot in front of the other, Louri eases toward the opening, leading into the dollhouse room. Turning on the light, she is blown away by Skyler's newest dollhouse—it's breathtaking. It's in such good shape to be an antique.

"Wow, an ancient barn-shape dollhouse," she says out loud. Taking a few steps closer, she then hears the ringtone from her phone, turning swiftly and then running into her old room to answer it.

"Hello," she says.

It's her roommate from college. After talking to her roommate, Louri takes off her pink fuzzy house shoes then places them on the floor by her bed and sits on the edge of the bed, closing her eyes and folding her hands.

"Now lay me down to sleep… I pray the Lord my soul to keep… If I shall die before I wake… I pray the Lord my soul to take," she says.

Boom, boom, boom! Opening her eyes instantly, Louri is startled by the loud noise. Jumping up and running toward the steps, she slowly eases one step at a time down into the foyer. Mysteriously out of nowhere, she sees a black silhouette dart pass her eyes. Stopping in her tracks as her thickset body tenses up, she can no longer move and standing in one spot. Her green eyes are spooked with fear. Then at that moment, she turns frantically toward the sound of the front door.

"Skyler, Mom, Dad, I'm so freaking glad you guys are here!" she says, holding her chest.

Rubbing her curly red hair, Amber can feel Louri's body tremble.

"Oh my god, baby, are you okay?" asks her dad.

"What happened? What's wrong?" asks her mother.

"I thought I heard and saw something," says Louri.

"Randy, do you think someone is in the house?" Amber asks.

"Let me check. You three, stay put," says Randy.

Randy pulls his gun from his gun holster and starts walking throughout each room downstairs of the large house, walking past the females as he cautiously goes up the steps, checking each room.

He reaches the dollhouse room and flicks on the light to see if there's anybody inside there. He notices that there is something bizarre about the new dollhouse. The windows and doors are all wide open on it. He slowly walks up to the dollhouse, closing the doors and windows on it before turning and walking back downstairs to the females.

"Should we call the police?" asks Amber.

"No, I checked the entire house. No one is here," he responds.

Later on, after the four have settled down for the night, Louri is sound asleep. A cold breeze comes over her body, walking over her to the bedroom door, shutting and locking simultaneously. Without warning, she spots a little boy standing at the end of her bed with a demonic grin on his face. His face is small and as white as a ghost. His eyes are completely black and shifting. Louri opens her mouth to scream, but no sound comes out. Getting up in dismay as fast as possible, she runs over to her window. She begins to fearfully beat on it. In a matter of seconds, it breaks. The shattering glass awakes her parents in the next room. They try to open her door, beating on it, jiggling the doorknob. Nothing works. Her dad runs to grab his gun.

"Louri, open the door now, honey," her mother demands.

The commotion wakes Skyler.

"Mom, what's going on?" she asks.

"Step back, honey!" Randy says in an orotund tone.

Shooting the handle of the door quickly, the door opens, and Louri is standing by the window in a cold sweat looking at them. She can't move. The little boy is only seen for a brief moment before he attacks her repeatedly, leaving her scratched, bloody, and throwing up. Her parents run over instantly hugging her.

"Are you okay?" Amber asks.

"Who in the hell was that?" asks Randy.

Running over to Skyler, who is still standing outside the bedroom door with his gun in his right hand, he hugs her close with his left arm.

"Daddy, who was that?" asks Skyler

"I don't have a clue, baby," Randy replies.

NOW YOU CAN LAY ME DOWN TO SLEEP

Just as it gets cold in the room, unidentified footsteps and a disembodied voice start coming from toward the far side of the bed. Randy raises his gun as the footsteps move closer and closer toward Amber and Louri. He fires one shot in the direction of the bloodcurdling sounds. Louri screams as she is swiftly snatched paranormally from Amber's tight grip.

"Louri, no!" screams Amber, crying. She watches as Louri is tossed quickly out the window and three stories down below, and just like that, the house becomes silent. Running to look down and out the window, the family is in shock seeing Louri motionless in the darkness on the lawn below. Crying, Randy calls the St. Charles County Police. They come in and proceed with an extensive murder investigation.

"First, a missing person here in this very house days ago. Now a murder or homicide," says the police. "Can't figure out if this a natural suicide or what. Regardless, we are going to have to ask the family to leave until this investigation is conducted," the police continues.

One of the police station detectives pulls Randy to the side.

"Hey, I am Detective Jason Albert with the St. Charles County Police Department, and we are going to have to ask you guys to go down to the police department then leave your home for the night while we do a full investigation on this," he says.

"Listen to me, this is stranger than you can imagine," says Randy.

"Randy, you have to realize these are two kids that are no longer here. One missing and one dead," he says.

"So you're going to make us leave our home? This killing of my daughter is the result of a supernatural being of some sort or something bigger I can't explain it," Randy says, before he strolls off to explain to Amber and Skyler, they have to leave for the night.

"Do you guys have anywhere to go overnight?" ask detective Albert

"Yes, my sister," Amber says, bawling her eyes out.

The family gather up a few items and prepare to go to Beaches's house. Skyler can't help but dread going over there even for one night. She hasn't seen her cousin since Cora's disappearance.

25

"First, we going to need you guys to go down to the station to answer a few questions, so don't forget, guys," says Detective Albert.

"It's the prayer ghost," Skyler murmur softly, looking up into Detective Albert's eyes.

Not responding, he's puzzled at Skyler's remarks. He watches as she walks and climbs inside her parents' car. After the family drives off, Detective Albert addresses his investigation team.

"Well, I have to gather up clues carefully, guys. I have a hunch the father may be behind this," says one of the investigators.

"I'm not so sure. He doesn't act suspicious enough in my eyes," says Albert.

Detective Albert starts his search upstairs since others are downstairs. Looking in the parents' beautiful bedroom, he notices nothing but does find the dad's gun. When he reaches Louri's room, an officer points out the bullet hole and casing from the gunshot Albert shot off earlier.

"This most definitely needs to be explained," says the officer to Detective Albert.

"Sounds like you have your prime suspect, Detective," Albert says sarcastically before laughing.

Detective grips Albert's arm firmly.

"Now you look here, Detective Albert. This is a very serious matter. If these were your two kids, this wouldn't be a game," the detective says.

"And you listen here, Detective, I am not underestimating anyone as a suspect. Meaning, I will get to the bottom of the existence, presence, or truth of who is behind this mystery," Albert says quickly snatching away.

As Detective Albert walks past the dollhouse room, the barnhouse dollhouse catches his eyes. Walking all the way into the room, he notices the dollhouse has one light in it on, and it was flicking on and off, bending down to look into the room with the blinking light. Albert sees no tiny bulb or explanation of the light inside the room of the light except its unusually bright. Suddenly he hears an eerie low voice of a boy.

"Now lay me down to sleep," the voice says, and Albert begins to unconsciously repeat the words.

"Albert, Albert," yells another detective, and before Albert could finish reciting the prayer, the voice vanishes, and Albert is able to think clearly.

"Are you okay, man?" asks the detective.

"Yes, I'm good," Albert says with no recollection of what has just taken place.

Raising up, Albert looks at the other detective. "I was coming to let you know that the coroners are about to move the body, and you may want to come to have a look at this," he tells him.

Albert rushes down and sees red marks all over the back side of Louri's body.

"Wow, how did that seem to happen?"

"Don't know," replies the detective.

"While you guys finish her up, I'm going to go down to the station and find out what the officers have found out from the family," says Albert.

The investigative team is combing the house one last time.

"Shhh, what is that?" asks one of the detectives.

The sound is a faint demonic voice that can be heard throughout the house. Each officer is confused.

"Now lay me down to sleep… I pray the Lord my soul to keep…" the voice says.

All the officers are unconsciously repeat the prayer word for word. Once they're done, they are all unaware of what has just happened and proceeds to do a quick sweep of the house one last time when, paranormally, the doors of the house began to slam shut and lock, the lights flicker and shut off. Scattered everywhere within the large home, the officers pull out flashlights, and they are all confused and wondering what's going on right now. The evil spirit inside the house starts to become upset and begins to torment the officers at the same time. Objects from different parts of the house are flying out their spots and hitting the officers one by one. A few officers are hit so hard and rapidly that they fall down from being knocked out.

One of the officers catches a glimpse of a small child as he dashes past him.

"Holy shit, this just got creepy," the officer says out loud to himself, turning his flashlight toward the direction of the figure, his gun drawn.

"Don't shoot, man, it's me," says a voice.

"Goddamn it, where are you, man? You scared the crap out of me," the officer says as he moves his flashlight over to the sound. Just then, his flashlight shines on a little boy positioned right in front of him. Frozen, unable to move or scream, the officer is paralyzed.

"Good night. You must die," says the spirit as he walks up to the officer and grabs a knife off the kitchen counter and slays him within seconds. The spirit vanishes as the officer falls lifeless with his eyes still wide open.

"Trent, is that you?" asks another officer creeping into the kitchen.

"No," says a deep, low evil whisper.

"Who's there?" asks the detective fearfully, and then his flashlight goes out.

The supernatural being appears within the darkness. The officer falls to his knees, grabbing his throat as he's feeling his tongue pulling as it is wrapping around his hands and throat, strangling him to death. The evil spirit then unleashes a horrific vengeance within the rest of the house, slaughtering the remaining officers and sucking them into the barn-house dollhouse.

Before I wake...

Chapter 4

Walking along the riverfront downtown St. Charles around the corner from the St. Charles County Police Department, Detective Albert is gazing into the waters on this beautiful day.

"You know, Sergeant Patty, I can't help think about how strange things are right now at the house in St. Peters after all seven of my homicide team police disappeared without a trace while conducting that murder investigation, and what's even more over the top is the out-the-norm events that took place that nights the girl disappeared and the night his daughter died," he explains to her.

"Where's the family now?" asks Patty.

"From my knowledge, they are to return home later today," says Albert.

"Maybe one of us could stop by to see if they remember anything else from that night," says Sergeant Patty.

"Well, in the meanwhile, I'mma see if I can do a search on the history of the home," says Albert.

"Excellent idea," says Patty.

Walking and getting into her car, Albert closes her car door and then smiles.

"I'll see you later," says Albert.

"Okay. I will be at the office while you're on your Scooby-Doo adventure," says Sergeant Patty then she cracks a smile winking.

CHERITA FORD

Albert laughs for just a few seconds and then waves goodbye as Patty drives off in her all-black Chrysler 300. Albert thinks Sergeant Patty is beautiful; he can't find one thing wrong with her. From her green eyes, blond straight hair, and petite curve body. When Albert was done investigating the history of the house, he heads over to see if the family was home.

"Hey, how's it going, guys?" says Albert.

"We're hanging in there best we can," says Randy, letting the detective all the way into the house.

"I'm here to let you know I didn't find any bad histories on this house," he tells them.

"What, no killings, no burial landmarks underneath the house?" questions Randy.

"Nope, nothing, so you guys be safe," says Albert.

"I think it would be clever if we keep searching for clues because something killed my daughter and a group of police officers and a little girl came up missing, and now the whole damn St. Charles and St. Peter's police force is looking at me and my family," says Randy.

"I understand your frustration, and believe me, I'm on your team with this," says Albert.

"Good, because this thing is bigger than me and my family can handle, but we're not running. I need to find out who or what in the hell killed Louri," says Randy, staring eye to eye with Detective Albert.

"Glad we are all on the same page with this," says Albert.

"Here's my card. Call me if you guys need or think of anything to tell me," says Albert.

"Yeah, yeah, sure, we will if we shall feel a need to," replies Randy, taking the card walking the detective out the house.

Saying bye, Amber, Randy, and Skyler are now back home. They settle back in after being away for a few days. Skyler is in her bedroom putting her things away.

"Hey, Mom, have you seen my charger to my cellular phone?" Skyler asks her mother, Amber, when she has seen her walk past Skyler's room and into her own bedroom. Amber doesn't respond. Skyler never sees her mom's face as she walks into her parents' master

30

NOW YOU CAN LAY ME DOWN TO SLEEP

bedroom's bathroom and closes the door. Skyler follows her knocks on her mother's bathroom.

"Mom, have you seen my changer to my cell phone? I can't find it, and my phone is about to die," she says after knocking a few times on the bathroom door. There is no answer. Skyler decides she'll go downstairs and ask her dad.

"Dad, have you seen my charger to my cellphone?" Skyler begins to say. "Mom, how did you get down here so fast?" asks Skyler.

Looking at Skyler in a puzzled way, her mom responds, "Skyler dear, we're clueless on what you're saying," says Amber. Walking quickly into the family room, Skyler sees her mother and father sitting watching TV.

"I'm mind-boggled because I just saw you Mom walk into you guys bedroom's bathroom, and you shut the door and turned on the shower," explains Skyler.

"No, honey, your mom has been sitting here with me since we've gotten home," says Randy, looking up at Skyler.

"Well, someone in your shower with hair and a body like Mom's," says Skyler.

Amber and Randy hop up to go check things out upstairs with Skyler. The three get to the room, and the bathroom door is open, and no one is in there. Randy walks over to the shower, and it's dry.

"Mom, Dad, I'm telling you, someone was up here. I've never seen her face, but she looked just like Mom," Skyler says.

Later on that night after supper, Skyler is headed down the upstairs hall, passing her playroom, when she hears giggling sounds coming from within the room.

"Cora, is that you?" asks Skyler, easing into the field with dollhouses. Slowly, step by step, she saunters all the way into the room.

"Who are you?" Skyler asks.

"Charlie," says the presence.

"Ouch," Skyler says, grabbing her head after being hit extremely hard in the head with a hammer that was sitting on her window ceiling.

"Skyler," says Amber, running into the playroom grabbing Skyler.

Skyler lies on the floor motionless.

"Randy, help, Randy, help me!" cries Amber, holding Skyler's head as she lay unconscious.

Randy rushes in. "What happened? Oh my god, Skyler," says Randy.

"Call 911," pleads Amber, not letting go of Skyler till paramedics arrive.

At the hospital, Randy and Amber sit at Skyler's bedside, hoping she wakes up and can be removed from life support.

"This house has ruined our lives. I'm horrified of what's going to take place next," says Amber with her face in hands crying.

"Yes, I agree. Things are out of control," says Randy.

"I plan to get to the bottom of this because my police department has grown impatient and wants to charge you," says Detective Albert.

"He hasn't done anything. You can't arrest him," says Amber.

"They can't arrest him, Mrs. Ford. If I thought your husband was guilty of anything, I'd already had him sitting behind bars a long time ago," says Albert.

Albert leaves St. Joseph Hospital.

"Hello, Patty, it's Albert," says Albert calling her.

"Hey, Albert, is everything all right?" asks Patty, picking up her phone.

"Actually, things just went from bad to worse for the Ford family," he tells her.

"Well, I will meet you at the family's home in about twenty minutes... What's the address?" says Patty.

"It is 0206 Greensboro Dr," says Albert.

Twenty minutes later, and Detective Albert and Sergeant Patty are at the family's home while they are at the hospital with Skyler.

"It has to be some truth to what the family is saying," says Albert, then right away, he and Patty begin to look high and low downstairs.

"You know this is exactly the type of lifestyle a family is supposed to have," says Patty.

"They work hard, buy their dream home, and are supposed to live the American dream," says Albert.

NOW YOU CAN LAY ME DOWN TO SLEEP

"Can you imagine what this family has to be going through?" suggests Patty.

Getting to the bottom of the steps leading upstairs, Albert pulls out his gun.

"Did you hear that?" he asks Patty.

Patty draws her gun and points it upstairs.

"This is the St. Charles Police Department… Identify yourself now!" demands Albert yelling upstairs.

"You stay here," Sergeant Patty tells Albert.

"No, let's go together, and I go first," he tells her.

As Albert guides the way, the detective and Sergeant Patty go upstairs at a steady pace, checking each room with caution, and nothing.

"Only in Missouri," says Randy.

"Hold up, what's that?" says Amber; without hurrying, she eases into the dollhouse room.

"Man, I know this kid loves dollhouses," Randy says.

"I see, but do you see that?" asks Patty.

"No, see what?" asks Randy.

"That," Patty points at the barn dollhouse.

Gawking at the dollhouse, Albert can't see anything when suddenly, out of nowhere, as soon as he sets eyes on, there are small footsteps coming toward them. Without warning, the other dollhouses except the barn dollhouse come flying at them without any human interference; they are swinging and blocking each dollhouse and its accessories as they fly hitting them. Ducking, dodging, the two get out the room fast. Once in the hallway, they run downstairs fast, trying to get away from the ruckus that has just occurred. The front door is locked. Then out of nowhere, they separate and a paranormal uproar begins. Looking around, all the power in the houses shuts off.

The supernatural being creep behind Sergeant Patty, and he grabs her leg. She falls, dropping her gun, slamming her face on the floor with a puddle of blood leaking out of her mouth. Detective Albert hears a loud boom, realizes it's Patty's skull slamming against the ground, and runs into the kitchen where the noise has occurred.

He quickly pulls out his flashlight then turns it on and sees her unconscious with a knife in her lower back.

Frantically grabbing for his walkie-talkie and dropping his gun to the floor, he says, "Officer down, help, please. Send someone now to 0206 Greensboro Dr. This is Detective Albert. Hurry, officer down," he cries.

Before he can pull Patty close enough, a long stool is sliding his way. He suddenly sees a spirit that whispers, "My name is Charlie, goodbye," in Albert's ear and bashes his leg in with a hammer he takes from the top drawer in the kitchen, shattering nothing but bone. Then Charlie walks away leaving them to grieve in the dark with their pain with no one to help. Walking away, Charlie giggles, leaving them and that little ray of light shining from the detective's flashlight.

* * *

"Now to add salt to the wound, I have a sergeant paralyzed in the abnormal trauma she's suffered," says Albert.

"I know, that's why it's time for us to get to the bottom of this and find out what's going on without police and anyone," says Randy.

Detective Albert and Randy go to visit the priest at the Catholic church.

"You know, while I was in the house, that barn dollhouse and the spirit said his name is Charlie. It was a boy," says Albert to the priest.

"Sounds like we need to do research on the dollhouse since the house history came up empty," says the priest.

I pray the Lord, my soul to take…

Chapter 5

"After all my research, I have found that this thing is evil, a very demonic ghostly force. It's a curse that began back in the 1800s. See, there was once the Minks family. There were six of them. The father, mother, and their four sons. The mother was beautiful, and all the small town New York women hated her because of it. Well, a local witch by the name of Nova was so envious due to the fact she lost the man of her dreams to Mrs. Minks. So the witch Nova cursed the Mink's family by casting a spell on the youngest child. This child's name was Charlie, and he axed his whole family and became a serial killer. If you say the prayer, you were dead. Pissing Charlie off will unleash him to kill anyone and everyone that says the prayer, and they will die. It's said he's also capable of provoking people to recite the prayer. Either way, he then kills them.

"To break the spell, we'd have to do an exorcism, but problem is, millions can die before it works, and if it doesn't work, billions can die. Charlie's spirit lives inside the barn dollhouse. What's more complicated about his death is because of a woman that was left to live when she was a child. The last massacre that caused Charlie's cruel death upset the girl, and grieving about, she cast a spell of her own on the house the Minks family lived and died in, shrinking Charlie's house, turning it in a normal-size dollhouse. The dollhouse was passed down on her family, but her family said she, too, died because of Charlie. She said the prayer, unaware that Charlie's spirit was what would have caused her death. After years of passing down generation to generation, the family hid the doll in the storage of an antique shop till up to a month ago," explains the priest.

The priest walks over, takes his finger, and makes a cross from his chin to his forehead and says a prayer before arranging to meet Randy and Detective Albert at Randy and Albert's house.

"Go ahead, Randy, leave Skyler's bedside to go into that house," says Amber, standing up from her hospital chair to stand beside Skyler's bed and then holding her hand.

"Say it, Amber, you think I'm a bad dad because I'm leaving my daughter's side to go check out what's in that house?" says Randy.

"Why do you want to go back there? The evil that exists in that house has taken our family from us," says Amber.

"I don't feel comfortable till this damn thing no longer exists," says Randy, hugging and kissing his wife. Then bending down, Randy kisses Skyler on her forehead.

"I hope she wakes up soon," says Amber. Wiping her tears from her face, Randy tries to comfort her best he could.

Later that day, Randy and Detective Albert go into the house, and the door locks.

"Wouldn't it be safer if we wait on the priest?" says Randy.

"Too late to think about that now, don't you think?" replies Albert, pulling the door shut behind them.

Just then, the house shakes for a few seconds. Albert looks over next to him and tells Randy it would be a good idea for them to stay together. Looking straight, he sees Randy standing upstairs.

Startled, Albert turns at the sound of the front doorknob turning. In walks the priest with his black bag in his hand.

"Where is Randy?" asks the priest.

"Good question, Priest. I think he's upstairs," he tells him.

They walk slowly up the steps.

"Randy!" yells Albert once they reach the top upstairs steps.

Just then, they both turn toward the knocking at the bottom of the steps. Suddenly the bedroom doors rip off the hinges and fly down to the floor. From the dollhouse room, they can hear Randy's voice.

"Now lay down to sleep, I pray the lord my soul to keep."

NOW YOU CAN LAY ME DOWN TO SLEEP

"No, Randy, wake up!" shouts Albert.

Randy stops talking and turns around.

"Albert, Priest, what's going on?" he asks.

"Get out now, or I will lay you all down to die," says a satanic voice.

"Charlie, you don't have to do this. You can let your soul finally rest," the priest yell out.

"How do you know my name?" asks Charlie in a low, bone-chilling tone.

"Now lay me down to sleep... I pray the Lord my soul to keep... If I shall die before I wake... I pray the Lord my soul to take," Charlie makes all three men unawarely recite the prayer together before they snap back to their normal mental state.

Jumping, looking behind them, the three men see Charlie standing with his arms down beside his frail figure, his zombie black eyes and dark, bowl-cut hair is accommodated by his ghostly white skin. The three of them back up and begin running in different directions. Randy runs downstairs and reaches to flick on the living room light, but a cold dead veiny hand is already present. Charlie takes his cold, veiny dead hand and grabs Randy around the neck, choking him till he can't breathe. Finally, once Randy is able to gasp a sound, he begins yelling and struggling to get away. Randy runs into the kitchen terrified and grabs a knife. The house trembles to knock the family's paintings off the walls. The light fixers shake, suddenly going out, and Albert, Randy, and the priest now are scattered separately throughout the eerie huge, dark house. Charlie is wandering throughout the house now with his ax in his hand, quietly pacing within the darkness, creeping up behind Albert in the upstairs hallway. Detective Albert has his flashlight out, and the gun is drawn, looking in the bedrooms, hoping to find Randy or the priest.

"Priest, is that you?" the detective says in a low tone.

Turning quickly, Albert is face-to-face with a demon Randy, pointing his gun straight at him. Albert quickly fires two shots. Then his flashlight goes out; he can't see anything within the blackness. Abruptly, Albert is struck by something and thrown against the wall.

"I can be whoever you want me to be," Charlie says.

37

Albert reaches for his gun as the light from his flashlight pops back on, lying, spinning on the floor. Charlie steps on Albert's hand, cracking and crushing his bones. Then bending down, Charlie squeezes Albert's hand and twists it till he hears it pop and break. Yelling in excruciating pain, Albert grabs his flashlight off the floor with his good hand. He swings the flashlight, hitting Charlie, dropping the flashlight. Getting up as fast as possible, Albert takes off running within the pitch-black darkness of the house.

Meanwhile, the priest is downstairs in the basement. He can hear the basement door and windows lock. From his long experience, his learned holy water is the best antidote for evil spirits, and he begins quickly dousing himself with holy water. Immediately on their own, his seven candles blow out.

"Dear God," the priest whispers faintly.

Unaware that Charlie is crawling at a slow pace toward him, the priest slowly but surely walks right up on Charlie. Charlie grips the priest's leg then takes both his hand and breaks his ankle bone in half before biting the priest's ankle with his razor-sharp teeth, and then Charlie slangs the priest across the room with the broken bloody leg he has a tight hold of. Getting swiftly, Charlie crawls up on top of the priest as the priest lies screaming, holding his bloody hurt ankle. Looking at Charlie in his lifeless pale, white face, the priest stops whining; he can't believe what he sees. Never has he ever laid eyes on such an unhumanly ugly creature in all his whole life. With caution, he takes his bottle of holy water and sprinkles a few drops of it on Charlie's face. Charlie screams with an unnatural tone for a few seconds before he vanishes. The floors start to shift back and forth, and the lights commence to blinking like a strobe light when in the kitchen Randy catches a glimpse of dark ghostly figure step toward him. It's Charlie... Randy holds his knife as tight as he can with his right hand. Charlie, without warning, grabs Randy's left hand, and then Randy stabs him. Letting go, Charlie swings his sharp, hard nails slicing Randy's shirt and stomach. Screaming, Randy takes off out the kitchen and hears Albert.

"Albert, is that you?"

"Yes," says Albert.

NOW YOU CAN LAY ME DOWN TO SLEEP

"He's behind me. He's coming," says Randy frantically and out of breath.

"Okay, let's go this way," Albert says then guides him into the family's farmer living room.

Once in the former living room, Randy turns on the light and turns toward Albert.

"You ready to die?" he says, laughing and then Randy began out of nowhere slowly turning into Charlie.

Charlie raises his hand, and without ever touching Albert, he tosses him across the room, making his body slam up against the wall. Albert lies unconscious.

"I am going to kill you until your soul reaches hell gates," Charlie says angrily, walking upon Albert, grabbing his hair and began pulling him dragging him up the steps.

Randy hides in the hallway bathroom, staring at Charlie as he pulls Albert into the dollhouse room.

Randy slowly creeps to the doorway of the dollhouse room; he watches as Charlie pulls Albert into the barn dollhouse, and they both disappear.

Randy runs down the step horribly frightened. He searches for the priest. Finally, he slowly opens the basement door.

"Priest," he yells down the dark steps.

"Yes, it's me, help!" the priest shouts.

Randy suddenly feels a shove, and he tumbles down the steps. He lands at the bottom of the steps in a great deal of pain.

"You okay?" asks the priest, not able to move from his leg being bit and broken.

"Yes," Randy says.

"Here, hurry. Get me my bag and candles quickly," says the priest.

Randy rushes over to get the items taking them to the priest.

"Get into the circle of my seven candles, hold this cross, and light these candles," the priest instructs him to do.

Randy does what the priest asks as fast as possible. After lighting the candles, he sees Charlie standing on the outside of the lit candle circle with an ax in his hand. The priest begins to recite a verse from

CHERITA FORD

Bible. Charlie becomes furious and in rage. The walls in the basement begins to close in at a slow pace. The priest keeps talking till Charlie looks at him and begins choking him without touching him. Taking the Bible from the priest, Randy begins to read and read fast. The priest, holding his neck with one hand, trying to stop the unseen from choking him starts to sprinkle his holy water on his neck with the other hand. Randy suddenly feels his body bleeding. Charlie is causing his body to be ripped open from a distance. With the walls closing in, the house starts to shake hard, the window breaks, and the doors slam on their own. Then the spirits of people Charlie had killed begin to float around, screaming in horror.

The candle blows out. Charlie appears in front of Randy and in the circle of the candles grabs him by his hand and pulls him to his knees. The priest then douses Charlie with holy water; Charlie is screaming a bloody evil scream so loud. Charlie disappears after his soul float up and away. The lights in the house come on. Randy is bloody but alive. He and the priest leave the house. Randy goes to the hospital with his wife, Amber, and daughter, Skyler. Then Skyler wakes up out her coma a few days later. The priest does a funeral gathering for Albert, and eventually, the family goes on to live a normal life.

The End!

Acknowledgments

First and foremost, I would like to thank the Lord up above for giving me life and always being my strength.

I want to give a big thanks to my eleven heartbeats, my kids, Dersean Ford and his two adorable kids: his son, Keanon Elvonté Hogans, and daughter, Kiarah Chayli Ford (a.k.a. Ms. Ford), Tia Broadway and son Zeramiah Ford, Delvonté Broadway, Chasity Broadway, her adorable son, De'Andre Blevins Jr., Staraesha Ford, her adorable baby boy Khyng Mcloud, Jerquise Nunley and her sweet baby girls Ava and Aaliyah Perez, Jernard Nunley Jr., Calvant Nunley, and Jervon Ford. I love you guys to the moon and back with every inch of love I have to give.

To my beautiful mother, Joyce Ford, and my 2 brothers Derrick Williams and Terry Lee Polk, I love you guys so much. Thanks for being great. To my brother Calvasean Ford (November 19, 1974, to September 21, 2000), you are gone but never forgotten. Thanks for being my angel, big bro.

My grandmother Erma Jean Polk, who passed away from cancer, I love you dearly.

To my soul mate Jernard Nunley Sr., who is a very strong, hardworking, caring man, I love you, baby, and hope to grow old with you someday. Thanks for being you!

About the Author

Cherita M. Ford was born November 5, 1975, to a young single mother by the name of Joyce Ford. She grew up in the inner city of St. Louis, Missouri, where she attended Walnut Park and Clay School Elementary. At fourteen, she moved to the suburbs of St. Charles, a city on the outskirts of St. Louis, Missouri. There, she attended the Francis Howell School District schools, Hollenbeck Junior High, and Francis Howell High School.

CPSIA information can be obtained
at www.ICGtesting.com
Printed in the USA
BVHW070738170523
664254BV00005B/529